Feisty Scholar Publications

www.feistyscholar.com

Spiral Fracture: First Edition

978-1-913619-10-7 (ebook)

978-1-913619-26-8 (Paperback)

Cover designed by Mibl Art

For news and details of upcoming publications from this author visit:

www.cherjones.co.uk

Chapter 1

The Friend

The pain medication dulled the throbbing in Rory's leg but had done nothing to ease the stabbing pain in his head.

'We're going to have to pin your femur,' the doctor said. 'A spiral fracture like this separates the bone into two parts.' The doctor stacked his fists on top of one another and then pulled them apart with a twisting motion. 'It often occurs when something stops you in your tracks, but the rest of you tries to keep moving.'

Rory pulled his hands over his face, tugging the skin down with them. 'That pretty much sounds like a metaphor for my life.'

'How did you say you did it?'

Rory hadn't. The last thing he wanted to tell this doctor, who was around the same age as him and clearly doing a much better job at 'adulting', was that he'd tripped over a kerb after a few too many. 'Football match.'

The doctor's eyebrows bobbed. 'I see.'

Rory was aware that the doctor could probably smell the alcohol on him, but the tightening in his temples was too distracting for him to care. 'I'm not going to be able to work, am I?'

'Not unless you have a desk job, I'm afraid.'

'No such luck.' Rory laughed because the other option was crying, and he didn't want to humiliate himself further. 'I'm a waiter. Or at least that's what pays the bills for now.'

'I've been there,' the doctor said.

That didn't help because Rory was very much *still* there and couldn't see the situation changing anytime soon. 'I'm going to write screenplays, though. At least, that's the dream. Sci-fi, mainly. Perhaps a little horror.'

The doctor gave him a polite smile that somehow managed to make Rory feel deluded, like a child explaining their plans to be a lion tamer.

Rory didn't blame him. He hadn't gained much, if any, traction in his career. Although his parents liked to tell him that they were rooting for him, just as often they reminded him that they would always find him a job if he decided to come home.

He'd hoped his luck was about to change. When the accident happened, he had been on his way home from a networking event. If he was honest, he'd gate-crashed it. One of the waiters he worked with had told him about the party and a service entrance he could sneak in through. If he was *really* honest, not a lot of networking had occurred either. He'd stood in the corner, gulping the first of too many free glasses of cheap champagne. A little courage was all he'd wanted, anything to stop the erratic swinging of his nerves. One moment he was terrified that he'd be noticed and asked to leave, frogmarched from the venue in front of the very people he wanted to impress. The next he was scared he'd remain unseen, another opportunity wasted.

As it turned out, the latter was the case. Not one person spoke to him until he tumbled over the pavement outside the hotel in front of a row of valets and waiting guests. To make his humiliation worse, he then had to wave away the offers of help to his non-existent car and limp off into the distance with his head hung in shame.

'Do you have family you could stay with?' the doctor asked.

Rory squirmed at the idea of calling his folks. Not just because he didn't want them to judge him, which he was certain they would do, but because they lived on a farm in the middle of nowhere. The idea of spending months there recuperating made him want to crawl on his hands and knees out of the hospital.

He didn't say that, though. 'Yeah. That shouldn't be a problem.' The pain in his head felt so bad that he could feel his pulse in his eyeballs. 'I don't suppose you could give me something for this headache, could you?'

The doctor frowned. 'Did you hit your head when you fell?'

'Maybe. I'm not sure.' It was that or the worst hangover of his life.

'Are you ...'

Rory was sure there was an end to that sentence and that he was supposed to answer. But it felt as though a rubber band were wrapped around his brain, filling his head with pain and his vision with a blinding white light.

Until, suddenly, the band snapped, and he was left in a dark empty nothing.

No white light at the end of a tunnel appeared. Rory didn't drift above his body or watch as doctors beat on his chest.

Instead, he found himself sitting cross-legged in the middle of a vast nothingness so black that he couldn't judge its dimensions.

He had a vague notion that he was supposed to wait for something, although he had no idea what. But he felt confident that eventually somebody would remember he was there and come for him. So he continued to wait.

After a while, he became impatient and decided to find a door on which to bang or a window to rattle. Rory picked a direction and began to walk. The spongy ground swallowed the sound of his footsteps. If there was any scenery around him, he couldn't see it change.

It might have been hours before he gave up. It might have been days. Still, he never reached an edge or brushed his fingers against a wall. So he sat back down on the ground and again he waited.

Then one day, he heard a woman's voice from above.

'Which one shall we read today, Rory? Well, if you're not going to pick, I'll have to.'

Rory reached a hand in the direction of that voice. Only empty air was above him. It was when he tried to drop it to his side that it brushed against a wall of earth. He turned in a circle, feeling out the dimensions of the narrow tunnel in which he found himself standing.

'This isn't possible.' Still, he grabbed a handful of dirt

and put it to his cheek. Just to feel something, anything, after so long brought a sob to his throat.

The earth was moist, as though a torrential rain had just fallen, leaving the worms within scrambling to the surface for air. Realising that dirt surrounded him on every side, Rory thought it would be sensible to follow their example.

The voice from above continued. 'This one's called 'The Friend'. Don't be deceived, though. It's not nearly as cheerful as it sounds. Ready?'

James sat in the corner of the doctor's office, struggling to hear what they were saying over Luke's chirping. He wasn't supposed to be listening, of course; however, it was hard not to when you knew you were the subject of the conversation.

'It's completely normal, especially for an only child,' the doctor said.

Mother clutched her handbag on her lap. 'It doesn't seem normal. You don't understand what it's like to reason with a child who won't accept they've done wrong. But then, why would he when he has an imaginary friend to take the blame?'

'Did you like the opening?' The woman's voice echoed down the tunnel of earth with such quaking volume that the walls began to crumble, spattering Rory's face.

Certain it was about to cave in, Rory dug in his fingers and climbed faster.

'I will take your silence as awe and continue,' the woman said.

'He'll grow out of it.' *The doctor patted the back of her hand.*

Mother won't like that, James thought. As if on cue, she bristled, shifting in her chair and smoothing her dress.

'So, there's no medication you can prescribe?' Mother glanced over at the corner where they sat.

James busied himself with examining the toys. Most of them were broken. Even if they hadn't been, they were far too young for—

'What?' the voice sounded irritated. 'But I'm on my break.'

Rory heard the sound of heels clicking on tile.

'No! Come back!' He scrambled up the wall of the tunnel, certain that at any moment he would be dropped back into the dark place (which, for want of more information, is what he'd begun to think of it as) with no walls, no light, no time. That or he would be buried beneath the earth that surrounded him. 'Please don't leave me.'

As if she'd heard, the voice answered. 'Sorry about that, Rory. Now, where were we?'

James felt like a giant. The rug on which he sat was printed with a spaghetti junction of roads which looped around him. He watched as Luke pushed a car along them, making the sound of screeching wheels as he circled a roundabout with a red and white striped tent painted in the middle.

'A roundabout is a stupid place for a circus,' James said.

'I don't think so.' When Luke was up to no good, he smiled with only half of his mouth, punctuated with one dimple. He put on a squeaky voice as he walked a Duplo character across the road towards the roundabout. 'I'm off for a lovely day at the circus.' Then he mowed the figure down with his car.

'We're leaving,' Mother snapped. Apparently, the doctor hadn't given her the answer she'd wanted.

The earth disintegrated beneath Rory's fingers so that he

had to dig them in deep, tearing his nails away from his skin. 'Keep reading!'

Luke headed straight for the playroom when they got home. James trailed after him.

'No mischief!' Mother called up the stairs.

In the playroom, Luke scrabbled under the bed. He pulled out a battered shoe box containing his treasures: a stone with a hole through the middle, a seashell, even the tiny skull of a bird. Then he held up something James hadn't seen before. A box of matches.

Luke struck one and stared at the flame until it burnt too close to his fingers, blew it out and reached for another.

Rory's voice was hoarse from yelling. 'Please! Can you hear me?'

He paused and stared upward, hoping for some clue that he'd reached the top or at least some notion of how much further he had to climb. He couldn't be certain, but a circular patch of the air above him looked a little more washed out than the all-consuming black he'd become used to.

Rory shoved his bare feet into the dirt. It squelched between his toes as he boosted himself further up the tunnel, until his fingers brushed that pool of not-quite black.

'Please don't,' James begged. 'Remember how upset Mother was after the flood? How much she worried about finding the money to fix the damage?'

Luke tore pages from a discarded storybook. He flashed his lopsided grin as another match burst into life.

There was no stopping him and James knew it. It was not as if he could run for help or overpower him. After all, there was only so much you could do when you were imaginary.

'So, what did you think? Be honest, did you see the twist

co—' The whites showed all the way round the nurse's wide eyes. 'You're awake.' She sprang to her feet, dropping her notebook to the ground. 'I need to get somebody.'

Seconds later, she returned, trailing behind a doctor. 'Is he going to be okay?' she asked.

The doctor shot her a glare over the top of his glasses, instantly silencing her.

'I'm Doctor Lewis.' He shone a light in Rory's eyes. 'Let me take a look at you.'

'Where am I?'

'The County Memorial Hospital. You've been with us for quite some time.'

'How long? Are my parents here?' Rory wasn't sure which question he wanted answered first.

'I'll ring them straight away.' The nurse backed out of the room, still gaping at him.

'You sustained a head injury,' the doctor said. 'It left you in a coma.'

Rory tried to fit the events of the previous day back together, but someone seemed to have filled the space where his brain used to go with cotton wool. 'I should ring work; I think I missed my shift.'

The doctor chuckled. 'I think they'll understand.' He patted Rory's hand. 'You'll be our guest for a while yet. Now—'

Rory's vision was flooded with red. He realised it was because the doctor was shining his light onto the outside of his eyelids. Although he didn't remember closing them.

'Rory, can you hear me?'

'Just so...tired.' Rory felt himself sinking, as though pulled through the bed and back into the earth beneath.

The last words he heard were the doctor's. 'We're losing him again.'

Rory settled back into the enveloping dark. Occasionally words reached him, but they seemed to come from every direction all at once. He would settle on a course, ready to follow the whispers out of the limbo he had found himself in, only to find those words echoing at his back, turning him in circles.

One day it was his mother's voice that he heard. 'Minimal consciousness. What does that even mean?'

'Mum? Mum!' Rory pawed at the air around him, willing the dirt tunnel from before to appear. He found only empty space.

'Exactly what it says. Rory scores very low on the Glasgow coma scale.'

'But he moved.' Her voice was thick with suppressed tears. She'd always been a proud woman and Rory knew she'd be doing her best not to cry. Not there, not in front of the doctors.

'Mrs Kelley, those responses are automatic. He's not in there any more. We have to consider his quality of life.'

'If you are suggesting what I think you are, you can forget it.' Rory could imagine his mother, head high, chin jutting out. This doctor, whoever he was, had met his match.

Rory didn't hear the doctor's response. The air around him seemed to thicken, dampening their voices.

He slumped back onto the floor. 'I'm still here,' he whispered into the gloom. 'I'm still me.'

Chapter 2

In This Life or the Next

It was that same voice. The nurse's voice. 'Okay Rory. I've got a new one for you. I thought you might appreciate the irony of it, considering your stellar sense of humour and current predicament. I've called it 'In This Life or the Next'.

The air around Rory had changed again. Before there had been only bleak, never ending space. But now it felt as though there was something just beyond the reach of his fingertips. He knew this in the same way he'd once been able to navigate his way around his bedroom at night without turning the light on.

Rory grappled around in the dark, looking for the wall of dirt. It wasn't there. Instead he felt the tickling prickle of leaves on his palms. He pushed forward. Branches blocked his way.

'Here we go,' the nurse said. 'I hope you're sitting...lying comfortably.'

'Please. Does it have to be now?' she asked.

'*I'm not heartless, Mrs Roberts. I feel for you,*' Remmy said. '*I really do. But crimes were committed, and they have consequences.*'

Mrs Roberts reached up from the hospital bed and clutched at her husband's sleeve. 'Do something.'

He opened and closed his mouth wordlessly. Then his eyes narrowed. 'You must feel really proud of yourself, harassing us like this. She's not long given birth. You know what you are? Bounty hunter scum.'

Remmy rubbed her temples. 'I've got a job to do, Mr Roberts. Try not to take it personally.'

Branches raked at the skin on Rory's arms so that he was sure, if he were able to see, he would find bloodied tracks blighting his skin.

A rustling behind him made him whip around. 'Is somebody back there?'

A guttural growl answered, so low it felt like it resonated through the floor and up into the soles of his feet.

Rory decided not to wait around and see what unseen creature shared the darkness with him. He pushed against the spindly limbs, ignoring the sting as they whipped at his face.

Mr Roberts spluttered, incredulous. 'You don't want me to take it personally?'

His wife began to sob. At first, they were silent little hiccups that made her shoulders jerk and roll. Then they turned to heaving cries. Fat tears rolled down her cheeks, landing on the little bundle in her arms. The baby stirred so that Remmy got her first sight of the wrinkly arms and legs as they windmilled from the blanket.

Mr Roberts rubbed his wife's back. 'What was the crime? Whatever it was, surely death was punishment enough?'

They weren't getting the point. They never did. Death wasn't the punishment. That was what he'd chosen to do to avoid the sentence passed by law. Life or death, his victim had never been given that choice. 'Murder. His crime was murder.'

Mrs Roberts stopped crying. 'I can't get my head around this,' she said. 'You're telling me that you're going to punish him for something that he didn't actually do. Something that a different incarnation did in a previous life. How is that fair?'

Rory stopped, worrying that he'd pushed so far into this maze of trees that he'd never find his way out.

It was a moist snort of breath on the back of his neck that sent him tumbling through the branches again. He scrambled onward, using thick boughs to lever himself forward.

Then he saw it, that same murky patch, rippling just out of his reach. He stretched an arm between the branches. Twigs poked at the side of his head and he pressed one eye shut against their assault.

Remmy hated this conversation. It was her personal purgatory, relived so many times it felt scripted. Every time she made an arrest, they dredged up the same argument.

Remmy drew a deep breath and began. 'Is it fair that the victims' families were denied justice? Suicide to avoid capture; he chose the coward's way out. The law is very clear on the matter. Justice will be served in this life or the next.'

Mrs Roberts' head snapped up. 'The next. Punish him in the next life. Don't take him from us now.'

Remmy shook her head. 'I've chased this one across

multiple timelines, spent decades tracking him down. He won't get away this time.'

Just as Rory got to the other side, teeth clamped onto his ankle, tugging him backwards. He winced in pain as they scraped against his bone.

'No!' Rory yelled as he was dragged into the darkness. But nobody answered. Nobody even heard.

Rory's fingernails raked in the dirt. He caught hold of a tree root and held tight, kicking his foot back at the thing behind him. Once, twice, it met with empty air. The third time it hit something hard and he heard the unmistakable yelp of a dog. *No, not a dog*, he thought, *a wolf.* He kicked back at it again. The jaw tearing into his flesh loosened.

On his hands and knees, Rory crawled beneath the mesh of branches towards the grey light beyond.

'Just give us more time.' Mrs Roberts began to sob again and this time the baby added its wail to the chorus. 'Please,' she said. 'A few years for us to be a family. Is that too much to ask?'

Remmy could feel her resolve begin to crack. She needed to get this done. 'It's not up to me. Besides, time wouldn't be a kindness. He remembers what he did now. As he gets older, he'll begin to forget the crimes he's being punished for. Now, give me the baby.'

'So, what did you think?' the nurse asked. 'Any notes or suggestions?'

Rory's eyes flickered open. It was so bright that his first instinct was to squeeze them shut again, but he had to ensure the beast that was chasing him hadn't followed him through.

'Where is it?' He tried to push the blankets off his body, but his limbs were weighted to the bed.

'Rory, calm down.'

'Where's the wolf?' Rory stared up at the tiny frame of the nurse. She wouldn't be able to protect them.

She put a hand to his forehead. 'It was just a dream. There's nobody here but us.'

Rory's eyes flickered around the room. Bright sunshine filled every corner. She was right. They were alone.

'It bit me. It bit my ankle.'

She pulled back the blanket covering his feet. 'See. There's nothing there.'

Rory struggled to lift his head. He managed it long enough to see that, other than a pink scar along his calf, his legs were fine. He willed his heart to slow and stared up at the ceiling. Plastic stars were dotted over the plaster. Rory knew that when the sun went down and the curtains were drawn, those stars would glow a soft green. They weren't quite the breath-taking constellation he'd hoped for when he and his mother had stuck them there. All the same, their familiarity brought a lump to his throat. He was home.

'How did I get here?'

The nurse blinked down at him. 'It's so lovely to see you awake again, Rory. Do you remember my name?'

Rory didn't think he'd ever known it. 'No.'

'You're always a little confused when you first wake up. I'm Caitlin.'

'I was in the hospital. The doctor told my mother there was no hope.'

Caitlin moved closer, tucking her blonde hair behind her ears. 'Well, it shows what they knew. Your mother had you moved here and employed me to help look after you.'

'Where is she?'

Caitlin gave him a tight smile. 'She'll be back soon.'

'My arms and legs don't feel right. Am I...' He didn't want to finish his sentence because then she would answer. If she answered, she might confirm that he wouldn't walk again, and he wasn't sure he could face that reality yet.

Caitlin must have guessed what he'd been about to say, though. 'I move you regularly, but some muscle atrophy is unavoidable. We can work on that.'

Relief left him tearful and Rory searched for a change of subject. 'I liked your stories. The one with the imaginary friend was my favourite.'

'You remember that?'

'Of course. I'm going to be a writer, too. When I... When...'

'Rory?'

'I feel strange.' The stars on the ceiling began to spin above him. 'Something's wrong. What is that?' Rory felt pressure across his legs. The blanket across them began to ripple. He tried to kick his feet, knowing already it was a hopeless task. 'Something's got me.'

Caitlin was over him in seconds, fiddling with the machines that he hadn't noticed before. He could see her mouth moving, but her words were lost on him.

Rory watched in horror as vines punched their way through the sides of his mattress. They snaked up his body and began to loop around him, weaving together so that it wasn't long before he couldn't see the blankets beneath.

'Help me,' he said, as they reached his chest. 'Too tight... can't breathe.'

As the vines covered his face and his world went black, Rory heard the distant howl of a wolf.

Chapter 3

Pivot

When the vines finally released him, Rory was back in the dark place. He sprung up, expecting the wolf stalking him to pounce. But all he found, at his feet, were the severed limbs of the vines that had entombed him. He picked one up and watched as it turned to dust on his palm.

At first adrenaline kept Rory moving. With every step he expected to hear the rustle of leaves or a threatening snarl. However, after a while, he began to think that perhaps Caitlin had been right. Maybe the wolf, the forest, all of it, had been some cruel hallucination. But still he didn't stop. He'd got back to the real world once. He could do it again.

Then one day he heard Caitlin's voice. 'Would you like me to read to you? I've been working on a few you might like.'

'Yes!' Rory walked in the direction of her voice. The slosh of water lapping around his feet stopped him. 'What is this?' One moment he'd been walking on the same old spongy blackness. The next the tops of his feet were covered in freezing water. At first, he was just curious, wondering where it could be coming from.

It was when it crept upwards, reaching his waist, that he began to panic. He'd often joked that he wasn't afraid of water, he was afraid of drowning. Some people had irrational fears that they couldn't explain. Not Rory. He could pinpoint the very moment his phobia began.

Aged seven, he'd been taking swimming lessons. The instructor allowed his students some free play time at the end of the session. Rory had wandered out of his depth and gone under. He frog jumped off the bottom of the pool, trying to get his mother's attention as she peered through the observation window, but she just waved in return.

He could only have been under the surface for seconds before the lifeguard pulled him out. But he refused to go back to lessons after that and his mother didn't make him.

'You're a fidgety one today,' Caitlin said. 'Maybe a story will calm you down.'

Rory patted at the air around him, hoping a tunnel or tree would appear, anything that would allow him to climb to safety.

'I've called this one 'Pivot',' Caitlin said. 'It's just a working title, so let me know if you have a better suggestion.'

The red numbers blinked, four taunting zeros. They rarely changed for Christopher. He'd watched with envy as friend after friend had bounded into his orbit, thrusting their own timer in front of his face.

'Amber!' they'd beam. 'At last!' Then they'd muse about what might await them as they watched the numbers begin to

count down. 'What could it be?' A wedding, maybe. Or perhaps a big promotion was coming their way.

Not that they actually wanted Christopher's opinion. They nodded without listening as he offered his suggestions, that same fixed smile on their faces.

Sure, he was jealous. There was no denying it. He felt it eating at his soul, like those little fish that would eat the callouses from your feet. So much so that, when their timers finally turned green, he found himself hoping it was something bad. An accident. Losing their job. Anything to remove those smug grins.

It wasn't something he was proud of. He hadn't always been like this. Once, he'd been just like them. Even when he had slept, he'd be listening out for the tell-tale ticking to begin.

Rory pulled in a deep breath as the water covered his head. As he sank below the surface, he searched frantically around him.

His hand touched upon strange skin that rippled like the turgid body of an eel. Rory snatched his hand back, repulsed.

Christopher could barely remember life before the Pivot watch. The smart phone companies had sold it as a wellbeing tool. A way for consumers to prepare themselves mentally for the big changes in their lives.

Time travel, of course, was illegal. But when the old men in wigs and robes had written those laws, they hadn't anticipated that the producers of smart phones and smart watches would be just that little bit smarter than they were. What they were doing wasn't time travel. They were just reading the resultant energy surges. It was no different from what the pre-cogs had been doing since the human race became self-aware, what most of us had once written off as intuition and instinct. The manufacturers of the Pivot watch had just found a way to patent and package it and sell it at a premium.

Torture, that's what they were peddling. For Christopher, anyway. He was in a constant state of anxiety whether his watch changed or not. Then, when it finally flickered to amber, he obsessed over what might happen. If it stayed a taunting red, then he asked himself why life was moving on for everybody but him. He knew the only escape was turning it off. But, like an abusive relationship, he'd become addicted to the anxiety it created because without it, he wasn't sure he'd be able to feel anything at all any more.

Rory's lungs burned. He ached to release his breath, to see bubbles float to the surface and to know that he could finally find peace.

He might have given in if it weren't for the feeling he was being circled. Something was getting closer, waiting for him to quit. When he did, Roy knew it would tear the flesh from his bones.

The first two pivot points he'd faced were anticlimactic to say the least. A small win on the lottery. A mediocre pay rise.

He'd prayed for something substantial, something truly life changing.

The third time it changed, it was. His father died. Nobody had predicted that. It took a long time for people to look him in the eye again. He'd like to think it was sympathy, but it was more likely they were concerned that such bad luck might be contagious. He'd become a cautionary tale.

The day everything changed, the ticking entered his dreams and yanked him out. Christopher blinked against the warm light filling his room from the glow of his watch. Then *he shoved his arm underneath his pillow, turned over, and pressed his eyes shut.*

Tick tick tick tick.

He squeezed his eyelids tighter.

Tick tick tick tick.

Still he could hear it. He snatched the pillow from the empty side of the bed and held it over his head.

Tick tick tick tick.

Christopher unsnapped the clasp and tossed the watch into the wastepaper basket on the other side of the room.

He lay back down. Seconds later, he jumped from the bed and snatched up the watch. He ran a thumb across the glass, relieved it was intact.

74:57 rolled over into 74:56. Just over three days and he'd reach a pivot point in his life, be it big or small.

'Okay,' he said to it. 'Let's see what you've got in store for me.'

The creature swam in ever decreasing circles. Rory could tell by the way its leathery skin slithered more often over his own.

Rory glimpsed the shimmering patch of grey in the depths of the water. He didn't as much swim as allow himself to sink beneath the creature coiling around him. His body felt like lead, but still his slow descent was excruciating as every fibre of his being screamed for oxygen.

Rory stretched out a foot and touched his toes into the pool of dull light.

That morning, Christopher pulled his sleeve over his watch. Whatever was coming, he'd face it. Not that there was any choice. What he couldn't face was the speculation of everybody around him.

He met Ellis in front of the elevator, jabbing at the button. 'I think it's stuck again. We'll have to take the stairs.'

As they puffed their way up ten floors, Ellis chattered away next to him. 'We can't be late. You know the Big Cheeses are looking to cut numbers. They'll take any excuse. Hey, are you even listening to me?'

Christopher tried to concentrate, but every few steps he was sure he felt the buzz signalling that his watch face had turned from amber to green. He kept pressing the cotton of his shirt against it so he could see the familiar yellow glow shining through.

'Can you keep a secret?' Christopher pulled up his sleeve before Ellis could answer.

'Wow! Congratulations! It's about time you got a break.'

'Yes, but we don't know it's a good thing, do we?'

'What do you—' Ellis flushed. 'Ah, your dad. Christopher, I'm sorry. I wasn't thinking.'

'Don't worry about it. But you said yourself, corporate are looking to let people go.'

'Not you, though. You keep this place going.'

Christopher shrugged. 'Nobody is expendable.'

Rory woke, gasping for breath.

'Just breathe,' Caitlin said, holding an oxygen mask in front of his face. 'That was quite the entrance.'

'What do you mean?'

'Well, you're usually a bit confused. But there isn't usually so much retching.'

'Sorry.'

'Don't be. That's why I'm paid the big bucks.' She settled down in the chair next to him and waited. 'Was it the wolf again?'

'No. I'm not sure what it was. You're probably right, though. It's likely just a figment of my imagination.' He didn't believe it, but there was no way to get her to understand as she sat in the safety of his bedroom.

'Yeah, well I'm wise beyond my years.'

He studied her through squinting eyes. 'Your hair's different.'

She ran her hand through the pixie cut. 'A terrible mistake. I was looking for the 'new me'. It turns out she has really bad hair.'

Rory laughed. 'I like it.' He didn't but saw no point in telling her that. 'Caitlin, can I ask you something?'

'Yes. But I can't promise I can answer.'

'Okay. I remember us meeting twice before. But there have been more times than that, haven't there?' The curve of her jaw, the line permanently bisecting her brow, even when she smiled, there was too much that was familiar about her for this not to be true.

She nodded.

'And me being here, awake, it isn't going to last, is it?' he asked.

She shook her head. 'Probably not. If the other times are anything to go by, we don't have long before you go to sleep again.'

Sleep. That was a nice way to put it. It sounded restful. Not the constant searching that had become his reality.

'I hope at least to see my parents first.'

'They'll be home soon.'

Rory noted the hesitation in her voice. There was something she wasn't telling him. No, something she *had* told him that he didn't remember. *Not now*, he thought. *That needs to be a problem for another time.*

'Finish your story,' he said.

'No, I...' Maybe it was pity that changed her mind, but she added, 'Well, I usually prefer my audience captive and unconscious, but I guess I could make an exception.' She flicked through her notebook. 'Where was I?'

They reached their floor just as the elevator doors opened.

'Typical,' Ellis said.

But as quickly as they'd opened, they began to shut. Manicured hands shot from between them and grasped the metal doors, pushing them apart. A woman slid from between them, sideways.

She rested her hands on her knees, gasping in deep lungfuls of air.

'Not another one,' Christopher said. Two people had already got stuck in that elevator this month. 'Miss, are you—'

The buzzing stopped him in his tracks. He pulled up his sleeve to look at his watch. Green.

When he looked back at her, she was doing the same thing.

Christopher glanced at Ellis, whose eyebrows bobbed suggestively.

'Shut up,' Christopher said, though he couldn't stop a warm hope from spreading in his chest.

'I didn't say anything,' Ellis said. 'Though, now you mention it, it's a bit of a coincidence that both of your watches went off at once. Hmmm, why might two people have a pivot point at exactly the same moment?'

Tick tick tick tick.

Christopher's watch sounded louder. He tapped on the

glass. 'I think it's playing up anyway so it's probably a false alarm.'

Ellis sighed. 'You need to open your mind to the possibility of good things happening, because...'

Tick tick tick tick.

Out of your league.

Christopher glared. 'What did you say?'

'I said it's a self-fulfilling prophecy. If you expect rubbish from life, it's what you'll get.'

Christopher forced his face into a smile, deciding he'd misheard. His friend wasn't in the habit of making cruel jokes. 'Well, I don't know about that, but as office manager, I guess it's my duty to check she's all right.'

He waved away Ellis's dirty cackle and headed towards the woman. 'Are you okay?'

She smoothed down her skirt. 'Yes. But I thought I was going to be stuck in there forever. I'm not good with enclosed spaces.'

He saw her eyes linger over his wrist and he shoved his hand into his pocket. 'Let me get you some water.' He led her towards the kitchen, sneaking little glances as they walked. Pretty, he thought, but high maintenance. Her heart-shaped face was framed by perfect waves. She sure hadn't sniffed her shirt that morning to check if it was passable before she put it on.

He handed her a glass. 'That elevator is a nightmare. Was this the floor you intended to get out on or just where the beast chose to spit you out?'

'Floor 10?'

Christopher nodded.

'Then this is my floor. I'm here for an interview.'

'Really? I wasn't expecting—'

'No, with Mr Carson.'

His boss. Why would he be interviewing somebody? Christopher mulled this over, not realising that she'd again begun talking to him. 'Sorry?'

'Emma,' she repeated. 'My name's Emma.'

'Christopher. I'm not usually so dopey. I didn't get much sleep last night.'

'No problem. If you point me towards Mr Carson's office, I'll let you get on with your day.'

'I'll do better than that,' Christopher said. 'I'll show you.'

They walked between the cubicles of the main office in silence. It was only when they reached the privacy of the corridor leading to Carson's office that she spoke. 'Look, I couldn't help but notice...' She looked pointedly at his watch. 'I think we turned green at the same time.'

'Oh really. I didn't realise.' He tried to sound nonchalant, but he'd never been a good liar.

She paused, as if waiting for him to add something. When he didn't, she said, 'Well, that's got to mean something, hasn't it?'

His cheeks burned. 'In what way?'

She tutted. Clearly, she was used to a more domineering type of man, Christopher thought. 'Look, here's my card. Give me a call if you want to discuss it further.'

He studied her business card, the letters of her name in a curly cursive and etched in gold. Emma Reynolds. He was tucking it into his wallet when he looked through the glass. Carson greeted her not with a handshake but an embrace.

Tick tick tick tick.

She wants your job.

Christopher spent most of the afternoon building the courage to call her. He'd rehearsed the conversation over and over. Still, he tried to dump the call on the second ring.

It was just luck that she answered on the first. 'Hello.'

'I'm sorry. I'm bothering you.'

'Well, perhaps you could tell me who this is, and then I can decide that for myself.'

'It's Christopher. We met today. You gave me your card—'

'I'm not senile, Christopher. It was a couple of hours ago. Of course I remember you.'

Christopher cringed, berating himself for calling so soon.

'So?' she asked.

'So...um...'

'So you were wondering if I'd like to meet you for a drink.'

'Yes.'

'At the Radisson.'

Christopher balked at the thought of the bill. 'Maybe the Traveller's Arms on Queens Road might be nice?'

'Okay. At eight o'clock?'

'Perfect.'

'I'm afraid I'm busy.'

'Oh...I—'

'Christopher, I'm joking. I'll see you there.'

When Emma walked into the bar, he regretted inviting her more than ever. Although, technically he hadn't. What was he thinking, inviting a woman of her class to a place like this? There was nothing wrong with it, but nothing right either. But designer shoes weren't meant for these tired carpets.

Tick tick tick tick.

Too good for you.

'Did you say something?' Christopher asked the guy next to him.

The man raised his eyebrows in return.

'Never mind.' Christopher stood to greet her. 'I got you a drink.' He thrust the glass of house white into her hands. 'I mean, hello.'

She beamed at him. 'You don't need to be so nervous. I don't bite. Shall we find a table?'

He followed her to a booth at the other side of the bar, first casting a smug smile at his neighbour. Yes, he wanted to say, she's with me.

'So, what do you think it means?' Emma tapped the face of her watch.

'Probably a coincidence.'

'Oh.' She took a sip of her wine, barely masked her grimace, and set it back down. Christopher kicked himself for ordering the house.

'Well, tell me about yourself,' she said. 'You seem to be doing pretty well at Carson and Solomon.'

Christopher rolled his eyes. 'Oh yes. Women love me and men want to be me.'

She took another sip of wine. 'You're funny.'

'Yeah, I'm here all week. So how did the interview go?'

'Great. I start next week.'

Was he imagining it, or was she avoiding looking him in the eye? Christopher pushed the thought away.

They chatted easily for the rest of the night. So much so that when she got up to leave, Christopher was surprised it had got so late.

'We should do this again sometime,' she said.

'That'd be nice,' he replied, assuming she was being polite.

'Only if you want to, of course.'

'I really do. That would be lovely,' Christopher said, a little too fast.

'How about an early dinner after work on Monday? I can tell you all about my first day.'

Tick tick tick tick.

Keep your enemies close.

That nagging doubt silenced him. What if she really was after his job? Maybe she was keeping him sweet so he wouldn't make a fuss as she slid seamlessly into his position.

'Christopher?'

'Sorry, I was trying to remember if I have anything on. But I think I'm free.'

When Christopher opened his eyes on Monday morning, Emma was his first thought. Yes, she was beautiful. Probably too much so for him. But her dry humour so matched his, maybe they were meant to be.

He tried to quell the hope he felt rising because he knew from experience that hope could be a dangerous thing.

Ellis matched his step as he entered the building. 'So, how did it go?'

Christopher didn't look at him. 'We had a very nice evening, thank you.'

'Come on. You've got to give me more details than that.'

'I'd prefer not to curse it.'

'Well, that sounds promising.'

Christopher didn't answer. They didn't bother with the elevator, bypassing the crowd waiting round it and heading straight for the stairs.

'I've got to meet Carson for the Monday briefing,' Christopher said as they parted ways at the top.

When he reached the office, he stopped. Emma was already inside. Carson cupped her tiny hands within his. They stood like that, exchanging words Christopher couldn't hear, before Carson slipped an arm around her shoulder and guided her towards the door. 'I'll see you here for a debrief at 5 o'clock,' he said, and closed the door behind her.

Tick tick tick tick.

It's him she's after.

'I thought we had a date tonight?' Christopher asked.

Emma jumped at the sound of his voice. 'Don't sneak up on me like that. It won't take long, then I'm all yours.'

'Really? I'm not sure Carson would be happy to hear that.'

'Excuse me?'

'Well, are you debriefing him or is he debriefing you?' Inside, any semblance of common sense or self-respect that he had left screeched at him to stop talking.

Emma turned on her heel. 'I don't need to listen to this. Stay away from me, Christopher.'

The door behind him was flung open. 'What the hell's going on out here?'

'It seems I've upset a mutual friend of ours.'

Carson's eyes narrowed. 'My niece?'

Christopher was running before his brain registered any plan to do so. 'Emma, I'm sorry!'

He caught up with her at the elevator. 'Please, I had no idea he was your uncle.'

'What did you think was going on in there?' She jabbed an accusing finger at him.

Tick tick tick tick.

Idiot. You've blown it.

'Shut up! It was you that made me think like that!'

Emma's eyes widened. 'Who are you talking to?'

'Nobody. It's nothing. Please. It was just a misunderstanding. Now I know he's just helping you out.'

'Helping me out? Nepotism, is that what you think this is?' She stabbed the elevator button again.

'Well...'

'How dare you? I got this job because I'm good at what I do.'

He put a hand on her arm. 'Emma, please. I'm sorry.'

The elevator doors opened. 'I said get away from me!' She stepped through the doors and into the darkness beyond.

She didn't scream as she fell. No blood curdling cry echoed around the empty elevator shaft. Christopher liked to think that was a sign that she hadn't registered what was happening to her before she hit the bottom.

Workers scurried from every cubicle.

'Christopher, what have you done?' Ellis asked.

'Me? Nothing. She just fell.'

As the crowds gathered around him, Christopher realised that he was standing on the very spot where he had met Emma. He rolled back his sleeve. The digits on his watch had turned back to red.

Rory spluttered as he suppressed a laugh.

'Nice.' Caitlin slapped the notebook shut. 'That wasn't quite the reaction I was going for.'

'I'm sorry. It was just the shock. She fell down the elevator shaft?'

'Yeah. It wasn't love that was going to bring them together. It was death.'

'That's deep.'

'Well, I'm the deep kind. Anyway, at least it cheered you up.'

'Please don't be offended. I think it's really good,' Rory said.

'I feel a 'but' coming on.'

'No 'but'. Besides, who am I to judge? Before my accident I spent more time talking about being a writer than actually getting on with it.'

'It's just a hobby.' Caitlin put her notebook on the table. 'Are you feeling better?'

'Yes. It's just...I know you tell me the creatures chasing me aren't real, but they're still terrifying.'

'I've been doing some research on lucid dreaming. I thought maybe if you could take control then you could banish whatever you think is after you.'

'How do I go about that?' Rory was sceptical but decided anything was worth a try.

Caitlin shrugged. 'Dr Google says you need to look for a sign that it's a dream. For example, a clock. If you're dreaming then the time will keep—'

'No good. It's completely black in there. If there is a clock, I can't see it.'

'Then how do you know you aren't alone?'

'Believe me, I know.' Rory pushed away the memories of the penetrating growl and the leathery skin.

'Well, that limits our options. Pinching your nose was mentioned.'

'Pinching my nose?'

'Yeah. If you can still breathe, then you know it's not real.'

'I'll try.' Rory thought back to the way his lungs had ached for oxygen. Surely that couldn't have been in his head.

'Just try to remind yourself that it can't hurt you.' She grimaced. 'Sorry. That's really easy for me to say, isn't it?'

'Yes. But then you can't see the water pooling at your feet right now.'

Caitlin jumped up, staring at the floor. 'There's nothing there.'

'Don't worry about it,' Rory said as he closed his eyes and waited for the water to rise.

Chapter 4

Fingerprint Auras

Two words. 'Fingerprint Auras.' That's all he heard Caitlin say before the buzzing began. The swarm moved as one, swooping so close to his ear that they sent him reeling, flapping at his own face. 'Get away from me!'

He imagined them, spiralling in the air above, regrouping as they readied themselves to dive again.

Rory crouched on the ground, covering his head with his hands. He felt the patter of little bodies as they hit his back. They left circles of heat behind, turning his back into a patchwork of pain, as though a hundred cigarette butts had been pressed into his skin.

Rory tried to think back to Caitlin's advice. The memory was fogged, as if that had been the dream, not this. His nose, that was it. She'd told him to hold his breath. He clamped his fingers over his nose and counted. He reached fifty and still there was nothing. No dizzying stars or gasping for air.

'This isn't real. You're trying to keep me here, aren't you?

Well, you can't stop me leaving.' Rory kept repeating those words to himself, although they did nothing to deaden the pain. He ducked his head against the onslaught and pushed forward.

It was only when the buzzing in his ears began to subside that he dared look up. There it was, his route back to the real world. His fingertips brushed the patch of ash grey and he stepped through into the light.

Rory felt exhilarated. He may not have beaten the force that lurked in the shadows, but his defiance had been a start.

It was something about Caitlin, as she frowned down at her notes before scribbling something out, that left him deflated. He couldn't place it at first. When it finally came to him, his face crumpled. 'I can't do this any more. It's so unfair.'

Her head snapped up. 'Hey, this isn't like you. What's happened?'

'It's just...your hair has changed.' The pixie cut she so regretted was now shoulder length. 'How long was I out this time?'

'A while.' She ran her fingers over the ends of her hair. 'I'm sorry. I didn't think.'

'It's not your fault.' He sucked in a steadying breath.

Caitlin dabbed his cheeks with a tissue. 'I'm glad my hairstyle doesn't have this effect on everybody.'

He didn't laugh. He couldn't. Still, she looked so awkward he decided to change the subject. 'I was thinking about your story.'

'You remember it? That's progress.'

'I remember all your stories. They're the only thing I recall with any certainty any more.' He felt as nervous as the first time he'd approached a girl at a school disco. 'The idea of it being destiny for two people to meet, I think that's kind of romantic. Even if there's a chance one of them will end up splattered at the bottom of an elevator shaft. And then I got thinking that maybe it was fate that we ended up here together.'

Caitlin blushed. 'It's time I changed this,' she said, fiddling with his IV line.

'I'm sorry. I made you uncomfortable. I wasn't talking about us. Not romantically.' Another lie. 'I just meant maybe it was fate you ended up caring for me. Medically I mean.'

'Yeah, maybe,' Caitlin said, not meeting his eye. 'Although, either way you're an easy patient. For one, you never bore me with small talk.'

Rory searched for a way to change the subject. 'Tell me another story.'

'That was a one-time only deal.'

'Please.'

Caitlin puffed out a long sigh. 'Okay.' She flicked through her notepad. 'This one's called 'Fingerprint Auras'. Don't blame me if it puts you to sleep again.'

The first words Blake ever said to me were, 'I'm not going to hurt you.'

Although, I knew that anyway. One of the few perks of my 'gift' was that I could usually tell when somebody wished me harm. But at that point I was so numb I'm not sure I'd have cared either way; I'd given up on the idea of life.

'I'm Blake,' he said.

I gave him the side eye. His aura was good, a calm sea green speckled with splotches of turquoise. That didn't mean he wasn't dangerous, though; sometimes the most dangerous people are the ones convinced their actions are for the greater good.

I took the sandwich he offered and tore off the clingfilm.

'And your name is?' he asked.

'Ali,' I said between mouthfuls. As I tucked in, it occurred to me that it was homemade. 'Was this your lunch?'

'I could stand to lose a few pounds anyway.' He'd sat down in the doorway next to me. I remember I didn't like that. I shifted as far from him as I could so that my shoulder was pressed against the shop window.

'A little cold to be sleeping outside, isn't it?' he asked.

'Thank you, Captain Obvious.' I felt bad as soon as the words were out.

'Yeah, I guess you wouldn't be here if you had any other choice.' He passed me a card. 'This place will give you some-where warm to stay. Short term anyway. My signature is on the back so they know I sent you.'

I eyed the little rectangle of paper with suspicion. 'Why do you care what happens to me?'

He shrugged. 'Why wouldn't I?'

True to his word, when I turned up at the hostel clutching that card, they welcomed me. I thought that would be it. A little respite and back to the streets.

So when Blake turned up at the hostel the next day, a hold-all of clothes slung over his shoulder, I was more suspi-cious than ever.

'These belonged to my son,' he said. 'He...he doesn't need them any more.' His aura dampened to a dull grey shot through with streaks of navy. The swell of grief that came from him threatened to overwhelm me and I looked away.

'Why are you being so nice to me?' I asked, rummaging through the bag. 'Are you some kind of social worker?'

'I'm a policeman.'

I stopped rummaging.

'An off duty policeman,' he added. 'And anyway, you kind of remind me of him. My boy.'

'Well, thanks.'

'No problem. I've arranged an interview for you at Vinnie's, if you're interested.'

'You've what?'

'It's just as a kitchen hand but it's a start.'

'I didn't ask you to do that.' My peripheral vision was tinted with strokes of orange, my own aura flaring.

Blake's had returned to the same serene calm. 'What's the problem? Do you have somewhere better to be?'

I didn't and we both knew that. Setting up that job was just the first in the line of things Blake would do to help turn my life around. I wouldn't say he was like a father to me as I didn't have a particularly high opinion of those. But he was my mentor. My friend.

It's not like I saw him every day but that didn't matter. His attention was constant and reliable, which was exactly what I needed.

Neither of us were particularly into deep conversations, so when one day he asked me about my family, it made me uneasy.

'I didn't fit in,' I told him. 'They couldn't accept the fact that I didn't see the world the same way that they did.' Although there was no way for him to know it, I was talking literally. When I'd first told my mother that I saw auras surrounding people she'd taken me to a doctor.

They'd given me pills and, although they'd never made the colours go away, I liked how they made me feel. A bit too much.

'Things change. Maybe if you gave them a ca—'

'No. They made it very clear that they never wanted to see me again.'

His aura turned a deep purple and began to spread as though reaching towards my own. 'Their loss. You're a good lad.'

I reached for my coffee to hide the glisten in my eye. 'Can I tell you something?'

He put down his own cup to show I had his full attention. 'Go on.'

'When we first met, I knew I could trust you because I could see it.'

'Thank you. Same here.'

'No, I mean I could literally see it. Your aura, the colours around you, told me the type of person you are.'

'And you see this around everyone?'

'Yes. Do you think I'm mad?'

'No, I think you're attuned.'

'A what?'

'A-tuned.' He split it into two drawn out syllables. 'It's what we call people who can see the magnetic field given off by living things. I'm no expert on the subject, but I've worked with a few people like you over the years. Most of them were empaths who had to work to read auras, though.'

'I don't 'work' for it. It's just what I see in people. Your aura is as clear to me as the brown of your eyes or the mole on your cheek. Do you want to know what yours looks like?'

He smiled. 'You're all right. I don't need a colour chart to tell me what kind of a man I am. You know, it's very rare a person is able to do it naturally. You have a gift.'

'Yeah, I'm blessed.' I thought of the taunts of my class-mates and the pleading of my father to 'just be normal'.

Blake took a sip of his tea. 'I could talk to my boss for you. Maybe he could get you some kind of advisory role.'

So that's how I found myself on the opposite side of a sheet of glass, the range of auras I saw spread out in front of me like the colour swatches in a Dulux shop. I sat with one of their officers, a serious looking woman called Halliday. I was surprised when she told me she was attuned too.

'None of what we see is admissible in court, of course,' she said. 'But it gives the detectives a good idea of which avenues to pursue.'

'I never imagined I'd ever meet someone else like me,' I told her.

'There are more of us than you'd think. We work in all sorts of industries.'

We went over the colours on the chart, noting which emotion I related to each. Halliday told me that the way they were linked was different for each attuned person. Where I saw grey as sadness or malice, she saw it as a calming neutral.

'Now we'll see what you can do,' she said. She stuck her head around the door and told the person outside that we were ready.

Almost immediately, the cell door behind the glass opened and Blake led in a suspect.

The interview lasted for nearly an hour. Blake fired ques-tions at the suspect, and after his response, I called out any changes in his aura for Halliday to note down. By the end I was listing colours robotically, my head buried in my hands.

Finally, Blake thanked the suspect for his time and stopped the recording.

'Are these interviews always so riveting?' I asked Halliday.

'I'm afraid not,' she said. 'Usually they're pretty dull.'

I jumped when the door to the office opened and Blake entered. 'How did he do?'

'Perfect score,' Halliday said.

'What do you mean?' I asked. 'I thought I was helping catch the bad guy.' I nodded towards the desk on the other side of the glass, but the man had gone.

He appeared behind Blake.

'Halliday said he aced it,' Blake told him.

The man walked towards me, hand outstretched. 'I'm Superintendent Reiner. It's a pleasure to meet someone so gifted. I hope you decide to work with us.'

He posed the question as though it were a choice. And I suppose on the surface it was. But when the other option was living in the hostel and bussing tables at Vinnie's, it kind of took the free will out of it.

So that's how I spent the next year, stuck in that claustro-phobic little room, reading criminals, their lies showing on their auras as clearly as fingerprints. It wasn't all bad. I managed to move into my own apartment and kit it out just how I wanted.

And, of course, there was always Blake, my own personal cheerleader. 'You're doing good work,' he would tell me. 'We're getting dangerous people off the streets.'

But I too felt as though I had been imprisoned. So when the head hunter came calling, is it any surprise I was tempted?

He followed me into the coffee shop. 'Alistair Rooney?'

'Ali,' I corrected. 'And who's asking?'

'Stephen Perez, but that's not really important. I've been asked to pass on the details of Courtney, Edwards and Lyle. They'd be very interested in working with you.'

For the second time in my life, a business card that was pressed into my palm was destined to change my life. Only this one looked very different to the last. The details of the law firm were delivered by embossed letters and surrounded by gilt edges.

It was Lyle that I met at my interview. I was nervous, and when I get nervous I say stupid things. 'Courtney, Edwards and Lyle; does that make you third in command?'

He didn't laugh. 'It's alphabetical.' He signalled for me to sit down. 'We've been told you're very gifted, Mr Rooney.'

'Yeah, so people keep telling me.'

'You don't see it that way.'

It didn't sound like a question, but I answered anyway. 'Not really. It's not brought me anything but trouble.'

'Well, we can change that. We would like to use your skills in rather a unique way.'

Little pulses of yellow, like static electricity, appeared in his aura. Whatever his plan was, it excited him.

'I don't much like the sound of being used.'

'I assure you, you would be compensated generously. All you would have to do is accompany our lawyers to court and tell us what you see.'

'Yeah, reading suspects is pretty much the gig I have already.'

'Oh no, you'll be reading the jurors.'

'Why?'

His aura swirled in shades of reds and purples. Waves formed from the depths before reforming into jagged angles. It was neither the colours nor the shapes that made me nervous. It was how quickly they changed.

'Our clients deserve the best defence they can. That's how our justice system works: innocent until proven guilty. We want to...root out any jurors who may not share our view on what is fair. That's something you can help us with.'

Explaining it now, he sounds manipulative, underhand. But I think that's just down to my storytelling. At the time, he was compelling. When I accepted the job, I even felt self-righteous. I was on a mission to ensure justice prevailed. The fat paycheck didn't hurt either.

When I told Blake I'd be working for a law firm he took it well. I softened the news by omitting some key details.

'It's an apprenticeship,' I told him. 'A chance to build on the foundation you all gave me.'

It stings to remember how pleased he looked for me. 'You'll be missed, but I always knew you were meant for bigger things.'

And so I passed the next six months trying to go unnoticed as I quietly vetoed jurors with scribbled notes to my colleagues. The judge questioned them. Do you have any preconceived ideas about the parties involved? Is somebody always to blame when bad things happen? Considering the details you've heard thus far, is there any reason that you couldn't be impartial?

The words that came out of their mouths were irrelevant. It was the tell-tale flickers of colour I was looking for.

Charges were read out as faceless defendants stood in the dock. Rape, murder, theft, assault, they all passed before me.

But I don't think I even considered what they were being tried for; like Lyle said, in the eyes of the law they were still innocent.

I didn't care, that is, until the day I felt Blake studying me from the other side of the courtroom. I tried to ignore him but I couldn't focus. When we'd adjourned, I found him in the corridor. 'What are you doing here? You can't just rock up at my place of work.'

'I'm a policeman. This is my place of work, too. I was the arresting officer.' His eyes narrowed. 'But while we're on the subject, what exactly is it you're doing here?' His aura was streaked with yellow flags of suspicion.

'Does it matter?'

He studied me so closely I thought this must be what others feel like when I read their auras. 'I'd say it does, yes.'

'It's all legit. I'm here to make sure they get a fair trial.'

His mouth hung open. 'You're rigging the jury. You have no idea what kind of an animal we're dealing with. Bennet's sick in the head.'

Up until that point I'd buried any guilt I felt under a layer of self-serving platitudes. But Blake had a way of making me want to be a better man, so it quickly surfaced. The problem with guilt is that it can put you on the defensive.

'Why don't you mind your own business? I'm not a child and you certainly aren't my father. I feel sorry for your son if this is what he had to put up with.'

He flinched and I knew I'd gone too far. 'You're right. I'm not your father.' He walked back towards the court but stopped to look over his shoulder. 'I was wrong, by the way. You are nothing like my son. When was the last time you looked in the mirror, Ali? How's your own aura looking?'

That was the last time I spoke to him.

I tried to focus on the case, but my mind kept wandering. The lawyer I was working with had to elbow me in the ribs several times, growling under his breath for me to get my act together.

Still, a week later I was celebrating alone with a beer in my apartment. Despite my poor efforts at vetting the jury, the defendant had got off. More than relieved, I felt vindicated. I'd had little to do with the jury selection process and still justice had prevailed. The system worked. How naïve I was.

My hand hovered over the phone as I considered calling Blake and trying to heal our rift. Tomorrow, I told myself.

The next morning, I was awoken early by hammering on the door. Reiner shuffled past me before I even had a chance to say hello.

'If you've come to have a go at me as well, please save it.'

His brow furrowed. 'I've got some bad news.'

I meant to ask 'what?' but no sound came out.

Reiner carried on anyway. 'Ali, I'm afraid Blake is dead. I'm sorry, I know you two were close. That's why I wanted to tell you myself.'

'How?' I regretted the question as soon as it was past my lips. I already knew. Don't say it, my brain screamed.

'Do you know a man called Gregory Bennet? Blake arrested him last year after he put his little girl in hospital.'

'I had no idea.' I meant about the crime. I knew the name well.

'Well, no reason you should. We see more of these sickos than I like to remember. Anyway, Bennet was found not guilty.'

'And he went after Blake?'

'No. To be honest, that would make this case a whole lot easier. Blake went over to his, I assume to warn him off hurting his girl.'

'And then what?'

'Well that's the question, isn't it?' Reiner said. 'If you believe Bennet and his downtrodden wife, Blake pushed his way in and attacked them. The woman has quite a collection of bruises to vouch for her story.'

I thought of Blake and his sea green aura. 'He would never—'

'Of course he wouldn't. But he was on private property without a warrant and we have only Bennet and his wife as witnesses. I'm afraid he'll probably get away with it, given the right legal team.'

'After everything Blake did, he was murdered.'

Caitlin shrugged. 'Yeah.'

'Wow. I mean, it was a good story, but aren't you supposed to be cheering me up?'

She slapped the pad down on the table. 'You asked to hear it.'

'I'm sorry. I really liked it. Honest.'

She took her seat next to the bed again. A hint of a smile tugged at the sides of her mouth. 'I may have overreacted a bit. You may have noticed that I'm quite passionate about my writing.'

'I like that about you. Did I ever tell you that I wanted to be a screenwriter, before all this happened?'

'Yes, you did. And you still could be.'

'Unlikely when I can't even hold a pen.' Rory felt grief begin to overwhelm him and, as self preservation, changed the subject. 'Maybe you could try a happy ending sometime.'

'Not my style. As a pessimist, life either proves me right or I'm presently surprised. It's win-win.' Caitlin checked the machines beeping around him.

'Are my parents coming today?'

'Oh sure, they'll be—'

'They're dead, aren't they?' Rory wasn't sure where the question came from. He hadn't even realised that he was going to ask it.

She'd been writing his vitals on a clipboard. Her hand froze mid stroke. 'I'm so sorry, Rory.'

He blinked back the gathering tears. 'When?'

'It's been a few years. Not that it matters, not when to you it feels like yesterday.'

'You've told me this before, haven't you?'

'Many times. It never gets easier.'

'No,' he said. 'I can't imagine it does. You know, I'm beginning to think that it would be kinder if I didn't remember them at all.'

Rory closed his eyes and for the first time he was happy for sleep to take him again.

Chapter 5

Every Girl a Princess

Rory only realised the crack was there because it was a hopeless matt black, blacker even than the nothingness around him. Somehow, he knew with certainty that this was the point where all of the light had been sucked from the dark place. He imagined it as a plug hole where all the joy and good had ebbed away.

Rory stuck a toe into it, feeling out its edges. It groaned a protest and the ground shook, sending him reeling backwards. When the crack began to expand, he scooted away from it. The tremors encircled him, leaving him no avenue of escape. They looped him over and over, the ground crumbling away so that Rory found himself sitting upon a pillar of earth.

'Enough,' Rory told himself. 'It's just a hallucination.' He crept to the edge and peered into the bleak nothing that had opened below him. If there was a bottom, he couldn't see it. Rory grabbed a fistful of displaced earth and dropped it into the abyss. No satisfying clunk echoed back at him, signalling it had reached the bottom.

He heard the growl first. It was quickly accompanied by a buzz. The sound of limbs sloshing through water was closest. The sounds rebounded at him from every angle.

Rory scoured the darkness. Nothing appeared, but he knew they were there, waiting for him to make his next move.

'I think it's time I took my fate into my own hands.' He stepped off the pillar.

If Rory screamed, he didn't remember. One moment he felt the whoosh of air against his face and braced himself for impact. The next thing he knew, he was back in his own bedroom, watching Caitlin sort laundry.

'Rory!' She dropped the sheet she'd been folding. 'You're back.' She pulled up short a few steps from the bed. 'I've been worried about you.'

'No need. I took your advice and faced the hallucinations. It worked. Maybe this is the start. Maybe I could be free.'

'That's great.' She hesitated. 'Do you remember what we talked about last time you were awake?'

'Yes.' Rory bristled with irritation. He didn't want to think about that, not when he finally had something to celebrate. 'My parents are dead and I'm all alone.'

'Wow. What about me? Aren't I always here for you? Besides, I think I should be guest of honour at that particular pity party.'

'What do you mean?'

'I'm alone too. I was scraping by when I met your mother.' Caitlin swallowed hard. 'She was kinder to me than any of my own family ever were.'

'I'm sorry. I didn't mean to upset you.'

'You didn't. Anyway, I've been thinking about your obsession with happy endings.'

'It's hardly a—'

'So I decided to put my own spin on a few classic fairy tales for you. It's called 'Every Girl a Princess'. Although, by the end of it, they might not want to be.'

'Oh dear. Why do I suddenly feel nervous?'

She just grinned in return.

'Nobody is going to see those?'

I was scribbling the occasional note on the pad resting on my knee.

'I mean, it's all private, right?'

I smiled back at her even though she had asked this same question several times before. It was the only contribution she had chosen to make so far. Each time she asked, I felt the whole group bristle. Even so, I didn't blame her. Caution was wise, considering her situation.

'As we discussed, this is completely confidential. You control which details you want to share, if any. And I use case numbers, not names, in my notes.'

As she nodded, her dark curls bounced. They created a stark contrast to her sunken eyes and pallid skin.

'Yes. Yes, of course.' She eased back into her chair. No, eased was the wrong word. Somebody at ease does not position her limbs to create the illusion of comfort, as she did.

Case number 1937: Although she had only recently been transferred to me, she had been in 'the system' longer than any of the girls here. She was a runaway. This was a common factor with so many of the women I worked with.

Not every story went as wrong as hers though. Human trafficking. She was being held captive in a home with seven men when the police found her, completely by accident of course. Nobody had been looking for her. Well, nobody that she wanted to find her, anyway.

The group holding her had been involved in illegal mining, which had led the police to raid the cottage she was being held in. It appeared her kidnappers weren't above stealing anything: money, diamonds, lives.

'Well, I don't care who knows my name. Belle. Nice to meet you all.' The interruption had come from the brunette to my right. She waved in a show of drama, though she had met at least three of the people in the room before.

'You're in high spirits today, Belle.'

'Why shouldn't I be?' She sighed, building up to the same monologue that I had heard countless times before. 'I really don't belong here. Here with these...' Her voice trailed off, but the unspoken word hung in the air as she glanced around at the other women. Victims. 'I'm sorry for you all; I really am. But I'm just not like you. I was happy.'

Case number 1991: Belle. 'The Diagnostic and Statistical Manual V' does not recognise Stockholm syndrome as a real psychological disorder. Well, I would love to invite its authors in to meet Belle.

Add to that post-traumatic stress and delusional disorders, and I would say she needed to be here as much, if not more, than any of the women I worked with.

Her defence of her captor, who held her prisoner for the best part of a year, made me uncomfortable. Not least because it made her such an easy target for further victim-isation.

'Belle.' I paused, choosing my next words carefully. 'You were held captive for months. Your father was there at your abduct—'

'Well, he's old. It was dark and he was confused. That. Didn't. Happen.' She rolled each word out before sitting back in her chair with her arms crossed over her chest. 'Maybe you're just jealous. Ageing, dried up; when was the last time you were even touched by a man?'

I ignored the insults. She needed to place the anger some-where, and until she accepted who the real target should be, I was strong enough to deal with it.

I was more interested in her suggestion of contact. She had never confirmed any sexual abuse by her captor. This was progress.

'You are always making out you're so much better than the rest of us. Well, you know what? You're pathetic.' Ella. The longest participating member of the group. And the youngest. It seemed wrong to call her a woman, but after her experiences, I couldn't describe her as a girl. 'Sure, we're victims, but we're survivors, too. Whereas you can't even accept that beast wronged you.'

'Okay, maybe a change of subject is in order,' I suggested.

'It's just so frustrating! How does she think—'

'Enough.' I said it as softly as I could, but Ella still looked as though I had slapped her. Any suggestion of disapproval on my part always hit her hard.

Case number 1950: Physical and mental abuse at the hands of her own family. Neglect. False imprisonment.

Now she was keen to please anybody who showed her

even the slightest bit of kindness. She turned her brightest smile to Belle. 'Sorry,' she said, before glancing back at me to gauge my reaction.

'We are here to support each other,' I reminded her.

I turned to Belle, keen to move the conversation onto less controversial ground.

'How are you settling into the sheltered housing?'

Belle didn't respond. She seemed captivated by a teacup that she now held in her hand, tracing a finger around its rim, lingering on a small chip. She laughed; a pretty tinkle of a laugh that came from nowhere.

Dissociative disorder. Her hallucinations provided a refuge for her in times of stress. They had been useful for her once and she was comfortable within them. But we had worked hard to break her reliance on them. I scribbled a note to ask her, at our next one-to-one session, if she was still taking her medication.

She glanced up at me, a flash of embarrassment colouring her cheeks as she realised she was being watched.

'I asked how you're settling in?'

'Fine.' She placed the teacup back on the table, the spoon rattling in the saucer. 'I like the room. It's blue. I always liked blue.' She didn't speak to me but down towards the carpet tiles.

'That's great,' I said with a little more enthusiasm than I had intended. I didn't want her to feel judged; she had survived the best she could in a horrible situation. Who knew how any of us would react in that same position?

Ella grasped at the chance to get back in my good graces after her earlier outburst, not that she had ever left them. 'The managers are really friendly. I liked it there.' After years of being passed around countless hostels, group homes and halfway houses, she was our resident expert.

I turned my attention to the slight woman sitting on my right. 'Perhaps our newest group member would like to share today?'

She toyed with the ends of the black plait that lay over her shoulder. 'Hello everybody. I'm Jasmine.' Her smile faded. 'I don't know what to say, really. I feel a bit of a fraud being here. You've all been through so much.'

I could see why she felt distinct from the rest of the group. Her tailored jacket and expensive jeans were a sharp contrast to the modest clothing of the others. She pulled her jacket tighter around her.

'Each of us has our own story. Yours is just as valid as anybody else's.'

Case number 1992: After resisting numerous attempts at an arranged marriage, Jasmine eventually fell in love with a local boy. He happened to be Muslim. This wasn't acceptable to her strict Hindu family and she had agreed not to see him again.

'I don't think I want to share today,' Jasmine said.

'Maybe she thinks she's too good for us.' A clear case of projection from Ella. She always looked presentable. She had told me that even when she had been homeless, she had sought ways of keeping herself clean – public toilets, shelter facilities when she could get access to them, shop restrooms if they would allow. However, there was no denying that the clothes she wore were faded and worn, little more than rags.

'You don't even know me!' In our one-to-one sessions, Jasmine had told me that she felt she'd spent her whole relationship defending her background, persuading her boyfriend

that she was not the 'Princess' he thought her. When she had broken up with him, he believed it was because she thought herself too good.

'And I hear you have some exciting news?' I hoped the change of topic would alleviate some of the discomfort she felt.

Jasmine had cancelled her last session with a brief email: her family had found her an appropriate match and she would be busy with marriage preparations. 'Yes. I'm engaged.'

'What's he like?' I found Ella's excitement at a blossoming romance promising: perhaps life hadn't knocked all the optimism out of her.

'He's successful. Very successful. He's been a work associate of my father for many years.'

I nodded my encouragement, but I felt unease creep over me. Why did I feel she was trying to persuade us?

'It's just...' she faltered, 'He's older than me. By a lot. My father's age.'

'And you want to marry him?' Belle asked.

'My family believe he is a good match for me.'

'That's not what she asked,' Ella said, voicing my own thought.

'He wouldn't be my first choice,' she admitted. The room was silent. She busied herself with fiddling with her plait.

'Nobody is passing judgement,' I assured her. 'We will support you with whatever choice you make.'

'Yes,' Ella agreed. 'Anyway, if he is kind, who cares how old he is? Age is just a number.'

Jasmine smiled her thanks before crumbling into tears. 'It's like he has my father under a spell.'

'Maybe we could talk some more about this in our one-to-one session,' I suggested.

She nodded, wiping at her tears with the sleeve of her jacket. 'I'd like that.'

I felt guilt begin to gnaw at the pit of my stomach as I looked into her trusting face. The reality was I didn't have some pearl of wisdom to share with her either here or at our private session. I could suggest charities and organisations that could guide her if she wanted to leave. But whatever her choice, it would have repercussions. The judgement of her parents. Possible disownment. Maybe worse. I couldn't guarantee her safety or that of any of the girls there.

As the session drew to a close and the minute hand struck twelve, the small party began to collect their things and leave. I watched as they began to disappear, one by one, into a world where I couldn't protect them. Not for the first time, I wished I had a magic wand.

Ella shrugged on her coat and rushed towards the door. She was moving so fast that she lost her shoe. She shoved her foot back into the ballet pump and carried on.

'Ella!' I called after her.

She stopped and glanced from me to the exit and back again. 'Sorry, it's just I can't miss my coach.'

'I just wanted to say I got a reference request through for you.'

'Oh.' She shifted, embarrassed, from foot to foot. 'I didn't think people really followed up on them. You don't mind? I should have checked with you first.'

Asking for help was not something she found easy. I waved away her apology. 'It's not a problem.'

'Thank you,' she said as she buttoned her coat. 'I'll see you on Tuesday.'

She had taken only a few steps towards the door before she stopped.

'You know, you've been like a fairy godmother to me,' she said, smiling back over her shoulder.

And with that she was gone.

'Human trafficking to Stockholm syndrome, that brain of yours is a scary place, isn't it?'

'Or maybe you're just naïve.' Caitlin sighed. 'So how are you going to use your newfound superpowers?'

'What do you mean?'

'Well, if you can recognise the difference between dreams and the real world, you could try and control what happens while you're there.'

'Is that even possible?'

'Google reliably tells me so,' Caitlin said. 'As a trained nurse, I might add I don't advocate the internet for diagnosis. But doctors are pretty light on the ground around here.'

'Everything is light on the ground around here. Jobs. People. Fun.'

'You have no idea.'

'I think I do. I was raised here.' He might have added that he'd left as soon as possible, but he was so grateful to see his little room every time he returned that the urge to wander felt alien to him now.

'Well, let's just say it's got no better since your accident.'

'Then why do you stay?'

'Your mother was kind to me. She gave me a home, and a friend, when I needed one.'

'Well, thank you,' Rory said. 'Caitlin, I want to ask you something and I want you to be honest with me.'

She shifted in her seat. 'I always am.'

'Am I ever going to be the way I used to be?'

'Well, it's going to take time.' She busied herself with tidying away her equipment.

'Look at me.'

If she'd heard him, she didn't respond.

'Be honest. Please. How much time?'

She took a steadying breath. 'I'd hoped your brain would adapt, that it would build different pathways, construct a new normal.'

'But it hasn't.'

'Not as far as I can tell. Sometimes I think we've made progress. Then you wake up and it's like you think we're meeting for the first time.'

Somewhere deep down, he already knew that would be her answer. Still, he couldn't help the grief washing over him. All his dreams, his plans, they were gone. 'Maybe that's a blessing. Remembering what I've lost is just too painful.' Rory closed his eyes and waited for the darkness.

Chapter 6

The Broker

'Newfound superpowers.' That's what she'd called them. Rory supposed that if he was stuck there anyway, he had nothing to lose.

He rubbed his hands together. 'Let's do this.' Then he started to run. After a short sprint, he jumped into the air. His feet barely left the ground and he stood there feeling foolish.

He tried again, this time leaping midstride. He landed heavily and fell, clutching his ankle. 'So stupid,' he said, slamming his fist against the floor, scraping the skin from his knuckles.

Rory rolled onto his back and stared at the endless midnight above him. Only it wasn't the uniform black he was expecting. A smudge marred it, like clouds covering the moon. 'A lot of good you are up there.'

Rory held his hand to his eyes, examining the scrape. 'If I'm not really here, then I didn't really hurt my hand.'

He watched, mesmerised, as the blemish evaporated.

'None of this is real.' He clambered to his feet, trying his weight on his ankle. No pain. 'This is my mind. I make the rules here.' He looked back to the grey patch above him. 'Maybe you aren't so far away after all.'

Rory didn't jump this time. There was no need. He decided he was weightless, and he was. Reaching his arms to the sky, he hooted as he lifted into the air.

Then he heard it: his own laugh echoed back at him. Although it contained none of the joy he'd felt moments before. It was crazed, desperate and wanting.

Skeletal fingers entwined his ankle, bringing his laughter to an abrupt halt. Whatever held him yanked downwards.

'Get off me. You're not even real.' Rory hoped he sounded more confident than he felt.

Suspended in midair like a child's balloon, Rory bobbed above the unseen monster below. He pawed at the air around him, looking for anything to stop his descent. Boney digits raked at his skin as it tugged him down. They made their way up his body until arms encircled him.

Then he felt something wet, sluggish, on his cheek. *It's tasting me,* Rory thought. *No, it can't end like this.*

But he had beaten death once before. Rory thought back to the little boy he'd once been, leaping from the bottom of the pool, refusing to submit, and knew that he couldn't give in.

Rory slipped from between the creature's arms and squatted down. Fingertips raked at his scalp as it searched for him.

Before it could grip him again, Rory sprung with as much power as he could, pushing his captor away. It wailed as he lifted from its grasp. Stretching his arms towards the freedom above, Rory refused to look back.

When he awoke, Rory was sobbing. At first, when he felt a weight upon him, he feared the creature had followed him back. But when he opened his eyes, it was Caitlin's arms that encircled him.

'Shhh, you're okay,' she said, her cheek pressed to his own.

When his body stilled, she lowered him back onto his pillow. 'What happened?' she asked.

'It was going to eat me.'

'What was?'

'I don't know.' Rory's words were snatched between heaving breaths. 'But it's real. The rest of it might all be in my head, but not that thing.'

Caitlin waited for his breathing to steady before she spoke again. 'Okay. So we know you can't run from whatever it is. And there's no hiding. That leaves only one option. You're going to have to face it.'

'No. I can't. Don't you understand? It will kill me. You've got to find a way to make this stop. Speak to the doctors again.'

Caitlin sighed. 'They've said there's nothing else that can be done. But you can do something. You can fight. Prove them wrong.'

Rory turned his face away from her. There was no way she could understand.

'Do you remember what you said to me last time?' she asked. 'About wanting to forget your old life?'

He nodded.

'Good. I wrote you a story. It's called 'The Broker'. I

hope it will help you see just how important it is to remember.'

I was very clear from the outset – No refunds!

Of course you are. Everybody thinks they are some special case that somehow makes them the exception. But rules are rules, after all.

Oh, here come the waterworks. Like nobody has ever tried that one on me before. It's usually followed by a tantrum when I don't give in. In case you really are as cliche as you seem, you should know I'm more than capable of defending myself.

Look, why don't you sit down? I'm not heartless, you know. It's just, if I let you have that memory back, I'd have to do it for everybody.

Ah, you're a quick one, aren't you? You're right; I haven't sold it yet. I don't usually purchase a memory unless I have a buyer lined up. But yours, well, I couldn't turn down a gem like that. Though, of course, you can't remember just how special it really was.

Why wouldn't I watch it? Don't give me that look. I paid good money for it. It's up to me what I do with it. I could watch it on repeat for all eternity or send it into oblivion. It's nobody's business but my own.

You know, I've been where you're sitting now. I was a seller in this business long before I was a broker. Birthday candles disappearing in a puff, surf lapping around my feet, my first kiss, all gone. When I try to bring those memories to mind, all I see are dancing lights like when you squeeze your eyelids together too hard.

The only reason I know that they ever existed at all was because I started keeping a ledger. I listed each memory I sold with the price I was paid for it printed neatly at its side.

I won't deny it; there was an initial unease. I worried that perhaps it wasn't just memories I was selling. Maybe those little snippets of my life added up to the essence of what was me. Like a much-loved patchwork quilt. I was worrying about nothing, though. That ledger was full and dog eared by the time I decided I didn't have much left to sell and perhaps a change of revenue source was in order. But look at me; I'm no worse for the experience.

Please, I don't need your sympathy. Just look around you. I want for nothing. Memories, my own and those of others, bought all of this. You would be surprised how much the rich and powerful are prepared to pay to acquire a memory without the effort that goes with it. Why go to the trouble of a bumpy trip across the Serengeti when you can download the roar of a big cat right into your brain? I doubt they give a second thought to the likes of you and me.

Of course we're alike. Answer me this. If it meant so much to you, why did you sell it? Yes, obviously money. But you must have other memories that you could have lived without. Anyway, that's none of my business. I'm sure you had your reasons, just like I did. Not that it makes a difference now. What's done is done.

Maybe you should start a ledger of your own. If nothing else, it will help you to keep a running total of the price you received. It soon adds up. In my rare dark moments, I like to run my finger down that column and tot up those figures.

Oh really? That's what they all say. But you'll be back. They always come back.

'You wrote that for me?'

'Yep. Do you understand what I'm getting at?' Caitlin asked.

'My memories are part of who I am. They're worth fighting for.'

'Exactly. As hard and for as long as you can.'

'I guess there's always hope.' He covered her hand with his own. 'Maybe if I beat this thing, we could make some new memories.'

She snatched her hand away.

'I'm sorry,' Rory said. 'That was stupid.'

She stood with her back to him.

'Please Caitlin, just forget I said anything.'

She sniffled and he was horrified to think he'd made her cry.

'I didn't mean to upset you.'

'This isn't your fault, Rory. You don't remember and I hate having to hurt you every time I tell you.'

'Tell me what?'

'When we first met, if you can call it that, I was a student nurse. I started reading to you on my breaks. You weren't even my patient. It was your name that grabbed me at first. Kelley was my father's name. He disappeared when I was a little kid. Not that I'm suggesting we're related. I just liked the illusion of having family that visiting you gave me.'

'You must have some family. What about your mother?'

'She was an alcoholic. I cut myself free from that particular noose a long time ago. It was just me and my little brother. I basically raised him. But we've gone our separate ways now.'

'That's a shame.' Rory wasn't convinced he really

believed that because, although he was alone as well, at least they were alone together.

'So when I saw your name written on the board outside that hospital room, I let myself fantasise just a little. Perhaps you were my father and the reason you'd never come back for me is that you'd been in a coma all this time. One day you'd wake up and we'd be a family.'

Rory spluttered, incredulous. 'That's stretching the imagination a bit, isn't it?'

'What do you mean?'

'Well, older brother, maybe. But father is pushing it.'

'How old are you, Rory?'

Time in the dark place was fluid, impossible to pin down to months or years. 'I'm not sure. I was twenty-seven when I had my accident.'

The sympathy on her face knotted his stomach. 'Could you get me a mirror, please?' he asked.

'Rory, there's no n—'

'A mirror, please.' He hadn't meant to bark the words, but his rising panic demanded that he not waste another second.

'I'll be right back.' When she returned, she held the mirror down at her side, just out of his view. 'Let's talk for a while first.'

'Give it to me, please.'

She handed it over and Rory held the mirror up. The eyes were his own, that much was true. They were the same hazel as his mother's. The rest of the face belonged to a stranger. Those familiar hazel eyes were hooded by heavy eyelids that he hadn't seen before, lines radiating from their edges. His once thick dark hair was grey and thinning so that he could see the shine of his scalp beneath. Rory turned his face away.

'I'm sorry.' She grabbed the mirror before he could drop it to the floor. 'I hate hurting you like this.'

'I want to rest now.' Rory pressed his face into the pillow, thinking that if the memory broker were here, he'd give him it all.

Chapter 7

Fragments

It was when Rory stopped caring if he lived or died that death tapped him on the shoulder. The smell of rotting meat, carried on rasping breath, made his bladder feel heavy.

'Enough,' he said, squeezing his urge to run back down into the pit of his stomach. 'I can't do this any more.' He turned to face the darkness and he saw the glint of two eyeballs looking back. 'If this is my head, then I choose to see you.'

The glare that filled his view did nothing to cloak the horror before him. The beast snorted through flared nostrils. Fangs poked from a muzzle that dripped saliva. It crouched back on its haunches, preparing to pounce.

'Come on! If you're going to do it, get on with it already.'

The wolf snarled but moved no closer.

'But you won't, will you? If you kill me, then you die too.' Perhaps that was why the creatures were so desperate to keep him there. If he escaped the dark place, one way or another, they might cease to exist altogether.

For a moment, Rory thought the wolf intended to prove him wrong. Its muscles shuddered below its skin, as though snakes writhed just below the surface.

Rory flinched but stood his ground. 'I'm tired of running. I just want it to be over.'

The wolf howled. At first Rory imagined it a victory call. It was only when he heard the wet tearing sound that he realised it was a cry of pain. The animal's skin had begun to split.

Tentacles weaved their way from the shredded fur, still grasping the wolf's innards. A limb weaved towards Rory and dropped its stomach at his feet, the contents spilling across the floor.

Bile burned Rory's throat and he swallowed it back down. 'What are you?'

The beast's mouth opened to reveal serrated teeth. When it roared at him, mucus splattered Rory's cheeks. He scraped it from his face, flicking it from his fingers. 'Why aren't you coming for me? I'm right here.'

It took a step towards him, its tentacles groping the air in front of it.

'You can't kill me because you're stuck here as much as I am.'

It hissed, but not at Rory, at something in the air above them. Its fish eyes widened as a buzzing echoed from every direction. A black swarm circled above their heads, before swooping down and blanketing them.

Rory slapped at the side of his head as insects scuttle across his eardrum.

He squeezed his mouth shut against the wriggling bodies that threatened to fill it. But still, bees pushed their way past his lips and into his mouth.

Scraping them away, he tipped his head back and screamed. 'Enough! You're not real!'

Rory felt the insects fly from his body. When he dared look, the beast opposite him had disappeared under the squirming mass of orange and black. But as they settled, it was a human form that Rory saw. The person beneath tipped back his head and bellowed with such rage that the swarm buzzed louder.

Some long-rusted cog in Rory's brain strained into motion. 'I know you,' Rory said. 'I know all of you.' He could see it clearly then. Fragments of films he'd studied spooled through his mind. 'You're just fiction.' The wolf-man, the tentacled mass, they were all just fragments of his memories, pieced together to torture him. 'None of you are real.'

The figure roared again, and the insects lifted from its body as a single entity.

Rory ducked down, covering his head as they looped around him.

When he dared look again, Rory let out a shuddering breath. Just as the others had been, the skeletal form in front of him was familiar. Translucent skin was stretched taut over jagged bones. Any flesh that the creature had once possessed had been eaten away by famine, illness or time. Most terrifying of all, when Rory looked into its hollowed sockets, he saw his own eyes looking back.

'There's hardly anything of me left,' Rory said.

The Rory-creature just blinked back at him. There was

no malice emanating from the wretched form, just a quiet despair.

'It's okay,' Rory said, holding a hand out to it. 'You can rest now.'

The creature mirrored his movement, extending its own skeletal fingers in return. When they touched, a spark of electricity bounced between them. It travelled up the arm of the Rory-creature, leathery skin flaking away as it passed. When the spark reached its withered face, the skin began to split, revealing a cracked skull beneath. It kept its gaze locked on Rory and, as the creature turned to dust, Rory sensed no fear, only relief.

As his heart began to slow, the world around him began to blacken again. It was only when his world returned to sweeping darkness that he noticed the light. It was distant at first, a twinkling star. But as his curiosity grew, it did too.

He was wary at first. That old joke came back to him, 'The light at the end of the tunnel is an oncoming train.'

But maybe it's not, Rory thought. Maybe it's just time to see which story comes next.

He still considered turning away, at least long enough to go back and say goodbye to Caitlin. But he couldn't help worrying that this was his only chance. Besides, he knew she'd be fine. His mother would have seen to that.

As if Caitlin had heard his fears, her voice echoed into the dark place. 'Night Rory. Things will seem brighter tomorrow.'

Yes, he thought. I'm sure they will.

Rory started walking again, but this time he knew where he was headed.

The Book of Jared

Chapter 1

Read on for chapter 1 of 'The Book of Jared', the first in the Escaping Sanctuary series.
<u>Escaping Sanctuary:</u>
<u>The Book of Jared</u>

This is the end. I do not blame you if you feel cheated. Nobody expects to open a book at the first page and discover that the story has happened without them.

I could have begun my tale with superstorms and flash floods. Perhaps you'd have enjoyed hearing of hail so big that it crushed cars or tornadoes that demolished cities.

But then I'd be cheating you in a different way. I was a small child when all of that happened. Climate change was whispered about over my head at the dinner table and reported on news bulletins that I wasn't allowed to watch. But there was only so long that they could shield me from such worries before they became my own. Though, I don't want to talk about that.

The day we were led below ground was the closing act. I stole a final glimpse of the rectangle of light as the door closed behind us. I would have looked for longer had I re-alised it would be the last hint of daylight I would see for years.

But every ending allows a new beginning, and that is where my story starts.

Edmond

The alarm blared, sending Edmond rushing from his unit. 'What's happening? David?'

'Give me a minute.' David spoke in frantic whispers to the security team, sending them racing towards the entry-way. 'Walk!' David yelled after them. 'And will someone please shut off that alarm! We don't want the citizens panicked before they even get down here.'

'David, what's going on?'

'It's nothing to worry about.'

'Don't do that. I'm not some doddery old man that needs your protection. Tell me.'

'Fine. We've had reports of intruders at the perimeter fence.'

'Is it them?' Edmond didn't want to dirty himself by saying the word. Cannibals. But that's exactly what they were. They'd already lost one team to them. Edmond had visited the scene and witnessed the devastation left behind. He'd owed that much to their families. After all, he'd sent them on that mission. But those images would be scorched into his memory forever. Bones stripped clean, discarded innards, he saw them whenever he closed his eyes.

'I don't know,' David said. 'But we proceed as planned. The guardians are going to patrol the boundary fence. There's no reason for the new arrivals to know anything about them.'

'Yes. You're right. There would be no point in scaring the citizens. It's just...'

'Edmond, what is it?'

'My family arrive today. My daughter, Laura and grand-son, Jared. They are probably up there right now.'

'Oh. You didn't say anything.'

'I already bent the rules by adding them to the list. I thought it best to let them go through the usual entry—'

'Edmond.' David cut him off. 'This place only exists because of you. Why shouldn't your family get a little preferential treatment.'

'I suppose.'

'No question about it.'

'You're right.' Waves of anxiety washed over him. 'I should have been up there looking after them from the moment they stepped off the bus.'

David clutched his shoulders. 'Listen to me. Earthquakes, floods, sandstorms, your family will have faced plenty of dangers without you.'

Edmond bristled. 'Is that supposed to make me feel better?'

'I'm sorry. That came out wrong. I just mean, they must be tough to have got this far. They'll be able to wait a few hours without you babysitting them.'

'But the intruders—'

'Are likely nothing but some survivors looking to see what all the commotion around here is. The sooner we get everyone below ground and those doors locked, the better.'

'You're right.'

'I usually am. Let the guardians handle everything up there. You just focus on your speech. I'll make sure your family's group is processed next.'

'Thank you.'

'And Edmond? Stick to the script. Please. The citizens need to know the rules as soon as they arrive.'

'I'll do my best.'

David grumbled. 'I guess that will have to do.'

Laura

'I'll never forgive you.' Those were some of Laura's last words to her father, and she'd said them at her mother's wake.

If she was honest, she'd enjoyed how he'd flinched as they struck. *Good,* she'd thought. *You can experience just a little of my pain.*

'There was no way for me to know. If I had any inkling—'

'What? You would have cancelled your trip, and I wouldn't have missed out on seeing my mother for the last time? Unlikely. You've never put me first.'

'That's not true.' Edmond's eyes glistened, but not a single stubborn tear fell.

Laura doubled down on her efforts. 'Or maybe it wouldn't have happened at all.'

'Don't.' It was a warning, but if anything, it just drove Laura on.

'After all, she'd have been safe at home if it wasn't for your precious work.' She could tell by the way his face crumpled that it wasn't the first time that idea had occurred to him. 'It's true. If you hadn't asked her to go with you—'

'That's a wicked thing to say.' Edmond picked up a plate of sandwiches. 'We have guests waiting. When you want to discuss this like an adult, you know where I am.'

'Hell will freeze over first!' That's what she'd shouted after him before letting herself out the back door.

Laura knew how cruel she'd been. Many nights she'd lain awake, wishing she could take those words back.

Now, she just felt foolish. Because it turned out that hell

didn't need to freeze over for her to speak to him again. All it took was a run-of-the-mill earthquake, barely a level four on the Richter scale. Nothing compared to what they'd experienced over the last few years. But Laura never imagined that as the ground stopped shaking that day, the earthquake would take her partner with it.

Laura pushed the memories down. She couldn't dwell, not when she had a child to protect. And if that meant swallowing her pride and accepting her father's help, so be it. But she supposed, considering that last conversation, she could understand why he hadn't come to meet them when they'd first arrived at the camp outside the Sanctuary. Still, it stung.

It was past midday, and still they squatted under one of the makeshift tents, waiting to be called. Thirty-seven, that was the number her group had been assigned on arrival. With painful slowness, they'd announced the numbers over the speakers. The last she'd heard had been number eleven.

'How much longer do we have to wait?' Jared had been asking the same question on repeat since they'd arrived early that morning.

It had gone past grating and Laura was gnawing on the inside of her cheek to stop from snapping. 'As long as it takes. There are lots of people that arrived ahead of us.'

'But they've been calling our number for ages.'

'What? No, that can't be right.'

Laura poked her head from below the tarp to listen.

Group number thirty-seven, make your way to the entrance.

'You're right.' Laura scrabbled around on the floor, scooping their things into her backpack. 'What happened to numbers twelve to thirty-six.'

'That's what we were wondering.' The woman next to her glared, her three children perfectly mirroring her expression. Laura could understand. They'd already been waiting hours when she'd arrived.

'It's probably a mistake. You watch, I'll be back in a minute.' She prayed she was wrong.

They joined a line of people. Although she recognised many of the faces from the coach, she'd exchanged little more than mumbled pleasantries with any of them. Now she beamed at them as the queue moved steadily forward.

'Is that the Sanctuary?' Jared asked. 'It's not very big.'

'Most of it is underground, remember.'

They'd camouflaged the entrance within a looming wall of black. Laura supposed it was a fitting choice for a mine. Still, she wished for some buttercup yellow or flamingo pink, already mourning the palette she would leave behind. It was a shame to be led through black into more black.

In contrast, the guards who stood securing the entrance wore a vibrant blue. They nodded as Laura's group passed.

A guide met them just outside the main door. 'I'm Jennifer, and it is my privilege to welcome you to the Sanctuary. I must warn you that the stairs are an original feature of Wieliczka Salt Mine. They have been checked and reinforced by the best engineers in the world. But still, I admit that three hundred and fifty wooden steps left me a bit wobbly when I first saw them.'

Laura glanced down at Jared, ready to reassure him, but she needn't have worried. He was standing on tiptoes, impatient to see what was inside. 'Come on, Mum.' She wondered if he'd be so enthusiastic if he realised all that he was leaving behind.

'Give me just a second.' Laura took a last look up at the sun. Born into the endless British drizzle, once it would have taken the slightest nudge of the thermometer for her to join the wave of people heading for the beach, shedding layers of clothing as they went.

But then, of course, the Levelling ended all of that. Humans no longer ruled; they survived. The sun had become a cruel master. Merciless, it hung above them, a constant threat.

For the longest time, Laura tried to secure herself and Jared in a bubble of denial. Switching the channel and leaving the newspapers unread let her believe, just for a little while, that they weren't quite as vulnerable as she feared.

Jared followed her gaze. 'Nicholas Copernicus – 1543. He was the first to say that the planets orbited the Sun. Did you know that?'

'I did not.' She pushed red waves of unruly hair from his eyes. 'Are you ready?'

'Yes.' He shook the hair back into his face.

'Then let's take a look at our new home.' Laura took a deep breath as they were led through the heavy metal door, into the unknown.

Jennifer hadn't been exaggerating. The steps coiled and twisted below, making Laura's stomach lurch. She clutched the wooden bannister.

'That's a long way down.' Jared sounded impressed rather than scared.

They began their descent, manoeuvering their bulky backpacks into the narrow stairwell.

'The original mine reached a depth of three hundred and twenty-seven metres.' Jennifer spoke into the gloom, her words barely reaching Laura, let alone the twenty or so people who trailed behind them. 'Looking at the entrance, you would have little idea just how far it spreads below Krakow. The original salt mine covered over two hundred and eighty-seven kilometres. However, during the construction of the Sanctuary, that number was more than doubled.'

At the bottom of the stairs, they entered a cavernous chamber of unpolished salt rock. Laura was surprised to realise it wasn't the crystal white she once scattered over her meals.

Wooden barriers lined the side of the chamber. Jared raced to look over. 'Isaac Newton – 1664.'

A huge drop still loomed below them. Nausea twisted Laura's guts, but she forced a cheery tone. 'Even I know that one, smarty pants. But I'm trying my best not to think about gravity, right now.'

'How far do you think it goes down?' Jared picked up a salt rock chip and dropped it over.

'I have no idea.'

'A good question, young man.' Jennifer stamped her foot. 'There is still a drop of over two hundred metres below us. If I were to take you to the lowest part of the mine, you would have to descend eight hundred steps spread across nine levels.' Laura's pallid complexion must have been clear despite the poor light because Jennifer added, 'Don't worry. You are perfectly safe. What you can't see are the tonnes of iron and steel supporting the structure from beneath.'

Jennifer directed them through one of the arches flanking the cavern and they found themselves in a tunnel. Laura let her fingers trail along the cool salt rock. Goosebumps rose on her skin, an enjoyable sensation after the endless heat.

The woman in front of them squealed and sprung back, landing heavily on Laura's foot. She didn't bother to apologise as she stepped forward again. Then she let out a chuckle. 'It's not real.'

Jared moved closer to her. 'What is it?'

Laura squinted to make out the two mannequins, positioned in a recess carved out of the rock. They wore white overalls, suspended for ever with their shovels scraping away at the ground. *Tough gig*, Laura thought. *Not even a coffee break.*

But to Jared, she said, 'Just a left-over exhibit, I think. In his letter, your grandfather said this place was used as a tourist attraction after the mine closed. I guess they were feeling sentimental when deciding what to keep.'

They continued down the passageway, peering at the tableaux staged in the recesses of the walls. The first figure stoked a fire, poking at faux embers that were backlit by an eerie artificial light. The next led a horse and cart, its hooves forever frozen mid-trot, a snapshot of a world alien to her.

At the end of the tunnel, Jennifer stopped. 'I'm afraid we have some final checks to do before you become official citizens of the Sanctuary. Nothing for you to worry about. It's all very routine.' Laura wondered if Jennifer was trying to persuade them or herself. By the furtive glances other members of the group exchanged, she could see they were wondering the same thing.

As they left the tunnel, the space widened, and they found a row of three desks. A clerk sat behind each one, checking the details of the new arrivals. Each citizen was processed and waved through with well-oiled efficiency.

Laura and Jared took their place in one of the queues. The woman behind the desk wore a silver name badge etched with the name 'Stacey'.

Laura heard raised voices from the queue to her right.

'But we've come all this way.' As the woman's volume increased, the pigtailed toddler clutching her leg buried her face in the material of her skirt.

'Just stand to one side, and somebody will come and speak to you.'

'No. No, I won't.' She squared her shoulders.

The clerk beckoned to the uniformed officers standing to the side.

One of them took the woman by the arm. 'Come with me, please.'

She paled. 'Just let us get settled in and I will come back and answer any questions you have. Or at least send Bella through.' She smoothed a hand over the back of the child's blonde head.

'We can't admit an unaccompanied child into the Sanctuary. Come with me, and we will get this sorted.' The officer guided her away from the line. The woman scanned the queues as she left, perhaps hoping for help.

Laura was embarrassed to be caught staring and looked away. Turning back to the desk, she realised Stacey was talking to her.

'Names, please?' The irritation in Stacey's voice suggested it wasn't the first time she'd asked.

'Oh. Sorry. Laura Pearse and Jared Morgan.'

Stacey tapped the names into a tablet. She scrolled through multiple pages and her brow knitted.

The people in the next queue were approved and allowed to enter. Then the group after them.

Laura gnawed at the inside of her mouth. 'Is everything okay?'

'Absolutely.' Stacey's smile was too bright, unconvincing. 'I just need to check something.' She waved over a man, and they exchanged whispers, throwing furtive glances back over at Laura.

'Is there a problem?'

'Laura Pearse,' the man read from the screen. 'And Jared Morgan. You have different surnames.'

Laura resisted the urge for sarcasm. 'Yes. His father and I weren't married. Is that a problem?'

'Well...' His incomplete sentence confirmed that it was. He flicked through further screens, before pausing. 'Your father is Edmond Pearse.'

'Does that make any difference?'

He handed the tablet back to his colleague. 'Welcome to the Sanctuary.'

Laura's heart picked up its regular rhythm. It hadn't occurred to her that they could still be turned away, let alone for something so irrelevant.

'One last task.' Stacey brought a stamp down, hard, on Laura's hand.

Needles punctured her skin. 'What was that?' Laura ran her thumb over the small lump it left behind.

'Your tracker. Everybody in the Sanctuary is required to have one.'

Laura looked closer at the stinging patch on the back of

her hand. A small 'S' lay in the middle of the aggravated skin. 'You can't just do that without asking.'

Stacey's smile didn't falter. 'I can if you want entry to the Sanctuary. You do, don't you?'

Laura looked at Jared. His fist was clutched around his father's lucky coin. He always carried it with him, holding it like a comfort blanket.

'Yes,' Laura whispered.

'Good. The boy next.'

'What? I'm not going to let you brand my child.'

'It only stings for a second. As you know.' Stacey looked at Jared. 'Besides, these chips are magic, so you'll definitely want one. It has a translator inside. You'll be able to talk to all the new friends you make, whether you speak the same language or not. Isn't that amazing?'

Laura knew Jared was listening, that later he would explain in minute detail his theories on how he thought the chip must work. But to Stacey, as Jared scuffed the toes of his shoes against the floor, it must have looked like he was ignoring her. Laura wished she had that option. Instead, she leaned forward and whispered to Jared: 'It's okay. I hardly felt it.'

Jared eyed her with suspicion. Laura didn't blame him. She had little experience with comforting him; that had always been Mark's area. Since his death, she'd stumbled from one clumsy parenting move to another.

To her surprise, Jared offered Stacey his hand. When she finished, he rubbed at the same blue tattoo. 'What does the 'S' mean?'

'STEM,' Stacey said, stamping each document on the

tablet with her thumbprint before flicking it aside. 'It's short for science, technology, engineering and mathematics.'

'Oh, there must be a mistake,' Laura said. 'I'm not a scientist or anything. I was a medical rep. I worked in sales.'

'I know.' Stacey raised one eyebrow. 'But your father is.'

Laura's face flushed at the implied nepotism.

'If you don't mind.' Stacey looked pointedly at the queue of people behind her.

Laura pulled on her backpack, but before she left the desk, she noticed a red 'T' on Stacey's hand. 'What does that stand for?'

'Trade,' she said, with a huff. 'Anybody who isn't in STEM research or a benefactor to the Sanctuary is lumped under the term 'trade'.' She screwed her lips into a pout.

'Sorry. I'll get out of your way.' Laura wasn't sure whether she was apologising for the delay or the unearned 'S' on her hand.

The Book of Jared

'Let's take a look at our new home.' That's what my mother said as we stepped into the gloom of the stairwell.

Our home. Those two words circled my brain.

Back on the surface, home had been so much more than four walls and a roof. It was built from the scraps of our history. It was stitched together with shared experiences and endured sorrows.

Home was not the three bedrooms and two bathrooms that we left behind. It was the footprints tattooed onto our front path. My six-year-old brain hadn't been able to resist the temptation of the wet concrete. To this day, I can feel the suction as it caked the soles of my shoes. I can still hear the squelch as I pulled my feet free, turning to stare at the footprints I'd left behind, panic rising as I realised they were not going to disappear.

When my father found me, hiding by the side of the house, he hadn't been mad. Instead, he planted his own shoes in the mixture right next to the outline of mine. 'Some things can't be undone,' he said. 'You're going to make mistakes. But when you do, know that you never have to hide them from me.' He pointed down at our footprints. 'No matter what, we're forever.'

So no, home wasn't the missing roof tiles or the peeling paint on the shed. It was the markings on the door frame that my mother had made on every one of my birthdays, my father and grandmother clapping me on as if I had any control over the outcome.

The home we once had wasn't defined by our untidy lawn, alive with dandelions and not much else. It was the cracked windowpane, which my parents had often talked of having repaired, that made it ours. I don't think they really wanted to change it at all. Discussing it was just an excuse to bring up my grandmother's attempt to teach me how to play ball. It was her that broke the window, by the way.

After I lost my father and grandmother, all that had made that house a home disappeared. The warmth and light that I remember filling those airy rooms abandoned us.

You could say that by the time we reached the Sanctuary, I'd been homeless for a long time. So it seemed as good a place as any to start again.

For more information on 'The Book of Jared', click on the link below or scan the QR code.
<u>Escaping Sanctuary:</u>
<u>The Book of Jared</u>